Moon Burger

Written by: J. Tatum, Jr.

MYND MATTERS

Copyright© 2021 by Jerry Tatum, Jr.

All rights reserved. No part of this book may be reproduced in any written, electronic, recording, or photocopying without written permission of the publisher. This is a work of fiction. Any resemblance to actual events or persons, living or dead, is entirely coincidental.

Books may be purchased in quantity and/or special sales by contacting the publisher.

Mynd Matters Publishing
715 Peachtree Street NE
Suites 100 & 200
Atlanta, GA 30308
www.myndmatterspublishing.com

ISBN: 978-1-953307-57-6 (pbk)
ISBN: 978-1-953307-58-3 (hdcv)

FIRST EDITION

For Rylie
Keep working hard and chasing your dreams.
You can do anything! And remember, you promised
to bring me a moon rock one day! :)

Chapter 1

It was a beautiful, starry, Saturday night. Rylie looked at the stars through her telescope, as she loved to do, while her Daddy grilled burgers on the deck in the back yard and whistled along to his favorite music–jazz.

A soft breeze blew the scent of the burgers to Rylie's nose.

"Mmm! Smells wonderful, Daddy!" Rylie said as she looked over her shoulder at her dad.

"Thanks baby! Should be ready soon." Her dad smiled,

6

That's when Rylie noticed something moving in the sky. She looked through her telescope to get a closer look.

Something was falling! Rylie turned the telescope towards the full moon and it looked like it was missing a big chunk!

"Daddy! I think a chunk of the moon came off and it's heading right for us!" Rylie said alarmed.

Daddy chuckled. "Oh! Don't be silly, Rylie. I'm sure the moon is just fine. See?"

Daddy looked up at the moon not expecting to see any problems but Rylie was right. A chunk was missing.

"Hmm...that's strange."

"Look! See that piece falling?" Rylie pointed at something that was quickly falling from the sky as it burst into flames. Her eyes stretched wide with excitement.

"I do see it, baby. But it probably won't come anywhere near us. Don't worry about it." Daddy flipped another burger and went back to whistling.

8

But Rylie did worry about it. She couldn't help it as the falling object seemed to get bigger and bigger as it fell.

It got closer and bigger.

Bigger and closer!

"Umm... Daddy! It's getting really close!" said Rylie nervously.

Daddy looked up and saw that Rylie was right. It was huge and heading right for the backyard but it was too late to run.

Daddy yelled, "Rylie! Look out!"

He dove on top of her to protect her. Just as he reached her, the thing landed in the backyard making a loud noise.

SPLAT!

10

The whole yard, the back of the house, Rylie, and her daddy were covered in sticky, warm, goop.

"Eww!" Rylie exclaimed as she shook the thick, yellowish, stuff from her arm. "What is it?"

Daddy stood up and his whole back was covered. A little bit of the goop had gotten on the corner of his mouth. He licked it with his tongue.

"I...I think it's cheese! And it's the most delicious cheese I've ever tasted!"

"Cheese?" Rylie asked confused.

"Yep! Cheese!" Daddy proclaimed as he got up and hurried back over to his grill which was also covered in the goop.

He picked up a goop-covered burger and took a bite. The taste of the goop blended perfectly with the burger making it the best cheeseburger he'd ever had!

"Rylie, you have to taste this!"

Daddy broke off a piece of the goopy burger and excitedly handed it to his daughter.

Rylie sniffed the piece of burger and inspected it before popping it into her mouth. Her eyes widened as she chewed.

"Wow! Daddy! It's delicious!" She exclaimed.

"I know! Everybody should get to taste this. Can you imagine? People would line up for miles to taste a piece of the moon!"

"Daddy, are you thinking what I'm thinking?"

"I bet I am! What are you thinking?" Daddy replied.

"I'm thinking we should open a restaurant and call it Moon Burger!" Rylie shouted excitedly.

"That's a great idea Rylie! Moon Burger it is!" Daddy agreed.

Moon
Burger
COME TASTE A PIECE OF THE MOON!
GRAND OPENING!
COME TASTE A PIECE
OF THE MOON!

Chapter 2

So, Daddy and Rylie opened a diner with a big sign in the front that said, Moon Burger! Come Taste a Piece of the MOON!

And Daddy was right. People came from all over the world to taste the moon! The diner stayed full of people from open to close and there was always a line outside the door that stretched for miles. Even different news channels from all over came to tell the story of how a piece of the moon landed in Rylie and Daddy's backyard and tasted so good that everyone had to try it.

The restaurant became such a big deal that even The President of the United States heard about it. He decided he wanted to try a Moon Burger for himself. So he, his wife, and his two daughters got in the Presidential helicopter, Marine One, and made a trip to the restaurant.

Once they landed, they all got out and got into The Beast, the President's special car. A long line of black cars drove through the city to Moon Burger. The President and his family waved to all the people in the long line that were waiting for their turn to taste the moon.

"We need to get in the back of the line and wait our turn like everyone else," said the First Lady.

So, that's what they did. Everyone was so excited to see the President! Special agents with dark sunglasses kept a close eye on the crowd as the First Family mingled with the other customers in line.

Moon Burger

COME TASTE A PIECE OF THE MOON!

GRAND OPENING!
COME TASTE A PIECE OF THE MOON!

Moon Burger

COME TASTE A PIECE OF THE MOON!

GRAND OPENING!
COME TASTE A P...
OF THE MO...

Meanwhile, back inside the diner, Rylie, Daddy, and their staff were working hard to make sure everyone got their Moon Burger quickly so the line could keep moving.

"Daddy! I heard the President of the United States and his family are waiting in line! Isn't that crazy?" Rylie exclaimed while serving a burger.

"Wow, I can't believe it! We'll have to make sure we make special Moon Burgers just for them!" Daddy replied.

They continued to work as the President got closer to the door. News reporters were all over the place!

"Mr. President, what brings you to our city?" A reporter asked the President as she held her microphone out in his direction waiting on his reply.

"Well, I heard about these fantastic burgers and I just had to come and see what all the fuss was about. And I'll tell ya...uh...I'm hungry enough to eat a horse!" the President said with a big smile.

"A horse and some vegetables!" The First Lady chimed in with a laugh.

"Yes, of course dear. Got to have those veggies," the President added.

The President and his family entered the front door of the diner with a bunch of Secret Service agents.

Rylie could barely hide her excitement!

"Rylie, will you go to the big refrigerator and get some more moon cheese please?" Daddy asked.

"Sure, Daddy!" Rylie hurried to the big refrigerator and opened the door.

"Oh no!" She hurried back to Daddy who was handing a to-go bag to a customer.

"Daddy?" Rylie tried to get her daddy's attention but the First Family was stepping up to the register to place their order and he didn't hear her.

"Daddy, I need to tell you something!" Rylie said as she tugged on her daddy's apron.

"Not now, baby. Can't you see the President is about to order?"

"But Daddy..." she said again urgently.

"Rylie, I said not now!" Rylie's daddy gave her a quick look that showed he meant business, so, she got quiet and waited.

"Well, hello, Mr. President, welcome to Moon Burger!" Daddy said to the President and shook his hand. "Thank you for coming so far to try our little restaurant! What can I get for you?"

"It's a pleasure to be here! I'd like to get moon burgers for my family and all of my secret service guys, to-go please. We're very excited to taste a piece of the moon!" the President said with a big smile.

"Well that won't be a problem, sir! Rylie, lets get these moon burgers started!"

"But Daddy, I've been trying to tell you something very important," Rylie said upset.

"What is it honey?" Daddy asked concerned.

Rylie whispered, "We're out of moon cheese!"

"I'm sorry, I didn't hear you." Daddy said as he smiled at the President.

"We're out of moon cheese!" Rylie said a little louder.

"Speak up, it's noisy in here," Daddy replied.

"I SAID WE'RE OUT OF MOON CHEESE!" Rylie shouted as loud as she could.

The whole restaurant got quiet enough to hear a pin drop. The President looked right at Rylie and said, "Uh...young lady? Did you say you were out of moon cheese?"

"Yes sir, we just served the last of it," Rylie said.

The President looked horrified and yelled, "NOOOOOOOOOOOOOOOOOOOOO!!!!"

WELCOME TO Moon Burger

Chapter 3

"Calm down, dear. I guess we just missed out," the First Lady said as she tried to comfort her husband.

"Well, this is just horrible!" said the President. "We're going to have to send our space shuttle crew on a special mission to get another chunk of the moon as soon as possible!" The President reached for his cell phone.

"Umm, Mr. President?" Rylie said shyly causing the President to stop in his tracks.

Moon Burger

"Yes? What is it young lady?"

"I don't think cutting off another chunk of the moon is a good idea."

"Really? Why not?"

"Well sir, the moon affects how and when the oceans move. And the oceans carry food around for all the creatures that live in them. If we keep taking chunks away from the moon, it will be smaller and it won't be able to move our oceans like it does. That could kill a lot of the things that live there!" Rylie looked serious.

28

"Hmm...go on," the President looked thoughtful.

"And not only that, the moon helps the Earth with its rotation pattern around the sun. A smaller moon could throw all of our seasons out of whack and many plants and animals on land could die too!"

"Oh my!" the First Lady said concerned.

"On top of that, have you ever noticed all those craters on the moon? Those were caused by asteroids and meteors that crashed right into it! The moon serves as a shield for the earth. We don't want those rocks making craters like that down here, do we? They could destroy entire cities!" Rylie exclaimed.

"Oh no!" the President's daughters said in unison.

"Who knows what else might happen if there was no moon?" Rylie added.

"You know young lady, you make some very good points. We better not go up there and mess with the moon," the President decided.

"Well, I do have an idea. Maybe instead of taking more of the moon away, we'd better fix it and make sure no more breaks off," Rylie said.

"Go on." The President waited to hear more.

"While the team is up there, maybe they can grab a few pieces of cheese that have already broken off, then we could have a great big cookout on the White House Lawn and everyone could have one last moon burger!"

"Plus a side salad," chimed in the First Lady.

"I like it!" exclaimed the President.

"Instead of everyone serving you, Mr. President, you, the senators and congressmen can serve everyone else. We can make it a big celebration because we fixed the moon!" Rylie said excitedly.

"Well uh... wait a minute there..." the President started.

"Rylie, I think that's a fantastic idea!" The First Lady gave Rylie a hug.

"Well, yes, it is a fantastic idea. Let's make it happen!" The President pulled out his cell phone and headed out the door followed by his family, the Secret Servicemen, and a crowd of reporters. All of the customers in line left too.

When the diner was empty, except for Rylie, Daddy, and the Moon Burger staff, Rylie's daddy looked sad.

"What's wrong, Daddy?" Rylie said, giving her dad a hug.

"Well, I guess I'm just going to miss Moon Burger," he said sadly.

"Don't be sad, Daddy. Something else will fall right into our laps just like the moon cheese did." Rylie smiled and kissed her daddy on the cheek.

"You're right, Rylie! Let's clean this place up!"

Chapter 4

One month later, the President sent a special team from NASA to the moon to repair any damage they might find and Rylie was right! There was another chunk close to breaking off. The team used their special giant sewing machine to stitch the moon back together and they grabbed some loose pieces of moon cheese to bring back for the big cookout.

Just as Rylie suggested, the First Lady organized the cookout and invited all of the senators and congressmen to come and serve the White House staff so they could feel special for the day. They all happily came, put on their aprons, and served the staff. There was plenty of music, dancing, and everyone had a wonderful time.

The President stood next to Rylie's dad as he grilled the burgers.

"Rylie is a very special young lady. I wouldn't be surprised if she becomes an astronaut one day and goes to the moon herself," the President said as he put his hand on Rylie's dad's shoulder.

"That's her plan, sir! She says she wants to be an astronaut and I know she can do it!" Daddy smiled proudly.

"Well, I believe she can do anything she puts her mind to. You should be proud." The President beamed as he walked back to the serving table.

"I certainly am Mr. President! I most certainly am." Rylie's dad grinned as Rylie danced with the President's daughters across the lawn.

TWO WEEKS LATER

Two weeks had passed and Rylie and her Daddy were on their deck in their backyard. It was another starry night with another full moon. Rylie looked at the stars through her telescope, as she loved to do, while Daddy turned the crank on their homemade ice cream maker. He whistled along to his jazz as a warm summer breeze gently rustled through the trees.

Rylie looked over her shoulder.

"Daddy, will the ice cream be ready soon? I can't wait! You make the best homemade ice cream!"

"Thank you, baby!" Daddy smiled. "I sure hope so, because my arm is so tired from turning this crank, it feels like it just might fall off!" He chuckled.

"Oh Daddy!" Rylie giggled as she went back to her telescope.

That's when she noticed something moving in the sky. She looked through her telescope to get a closer look. Something was falling just like before! But this time, it wasn't coming from the moon. It was coming from the stars!

"Umm...Daddy? Something else is falling from the sky and it's coming right for us again!" Rylie exclaimed

"Silly kid! What are the odds of something falling from space and landing in our backyard again? Things fall from space all the time. It will probably land hundreds of miles from here. Don't worry about it." Daddy laughed.

But Rylie did worry about it. She couldn't help it as the falling thing seemed to get bigger and bigger as it fell. It got closer and bigger. Bigger and closer!

"Umm...Daddy! It's getting really close!" yelled Rylie.

Daddy looked up and saw that Rylie was right. It was huge and heading right for the backyard again just like Rylie said. It was too late to run!

Daddy yelled, "Rylie! Look out!"

He dove on top of her to protect her from the falling thing. Just as he got there, it landed in the backyard, making a loud noise.

SPLOOSH!

The whole yard, the back of the house, and Rylie and her daddy were covered in cool, creamy glop!

"Eww!" Rylie said as she shook the creamy, whitish, stuff from her arm. "What is it?"

Daddy stood up and his whole back was covered. A little bit of the glop had gotten on the corner of his mouth. He licked at it with his tongue.

"Mmm! I think it's some sort of... milk. It's sweet, creamy, and the most delicious milk I've ever tasted!" Daddy exclaimed as he waded through the glop to the ice cream maker.

"Milk?" Rylie asked confused.

"Yep! Sweet, creamy, milk!" Daddy said excitedly.

The glop was dripping from everything and even got into the ice cream maker. Daddy dipped his finger in the cold bucket to taste how his ice cream would mix with the creamy glop. He put his finger in his mouth and jumped up and down.

"Rylie, you have to taste this!" Daddy dipped a spoon in the ice cream and excitedly handed it to Rylie.

Rylie eyed the spoon full of ice cream suspiciously before finally tasting it. Her eyes widened.

"Wow! Daddy! It's delicious!"

"I know! Everybody should get to taste this. Can you imagine? People would line up for miles to taste ice cream made with milk from the stars."

"Daddy, are you thinking what I'm thinking?" Rylie asked.

"I bet I am! What are you thinking?" Daddy replied.

"I'm thinking we can turn Moon Burger into an ice cream parlor and we could call it..." Rylie paused as she and her daddy thought for a minute.

Then, they both smiled and became excited at the same time.

"Milky Way Shakes!" They said in unison.

Rylie jumped in the air and gave her daddy a high five!

The End

CPSIA information can be obtained
at www.ICGtesting.com
Printed in the USA
BVHW052048310521
608491BV00008B/1697